D1313481

THE
OGRE

Written by Deborah Bawden

Illustrated by Xing Song

Collins

The Lady Eleanor Holles School
177 Uxbridge Road
Hampton Hill TW12 1BD

1 Rain

For as long as the villagers could remember, life had
been hard. The rain hadn't fallen for many years
and the sun sucked the moisture out
of the crops. The plants wilted
in the heat and died before
giving any fruit.

The villagers blamed it on the ogre
who lived in the mountains
towering above the village.
The ogre was spiteful
and greedy. He captured
the rain before it
reached the fields below
and drank it himself, and then
blew the clouds away.

3

Mama Bongani had predicted that two brothers with an unbreakable bond would defeat the ogre and bring back the rain to the village. Every time a boy was born, the villagers watched for some sign that he'd be the brave, strong warrior who'd defeat the ogre.

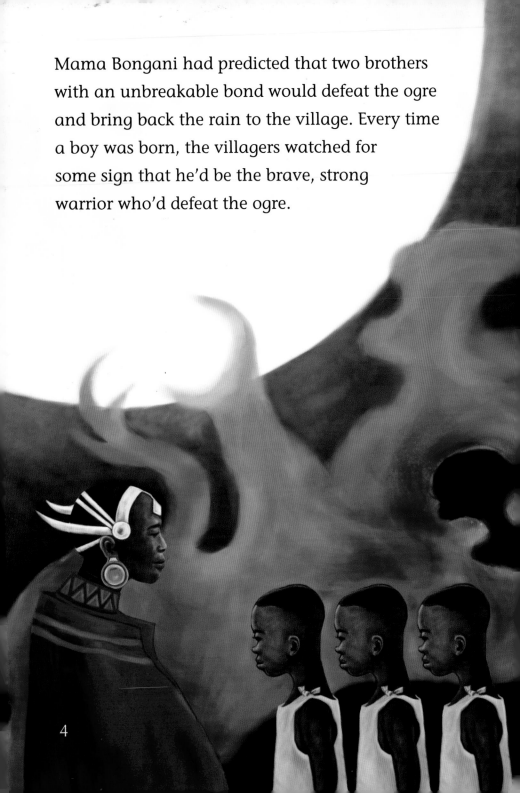

One of the villagers, called Sipho, was a brave hunter. The ogre had eaten many of the wild animals that lived in the shadow of the mountain, so Sipho walked many miles to hunt. But he always made sure that there was some food for all the villagers to share.

"Thank you, Sipho, for the gift of food," the villagers would say, when he came back safely. "May you have many children who'll look after you in your old age."

Time passed, and Sipho's wife Zandile was going to have a baby. Mama Bongani took one look at how big Zandile was getting and gasped, "Eh, Zandile, are you sure you've not got an elephant inside you?"

But it wasn't an elephant. When the moon was full, Zandile gave birth to beautiful twin boys. They were called Lindani and Busani.

Mama Bongani knew the boys were going to be special, because that night rain fell on the village.

2 The hunt

Eleven years later Lindani padded along the dusty path, carrying a bag of roots, herbs and leaves on his back. His hair stood up in tufts, filled with bits of leaves and bark. As his feet silently met the bare ground, puffs of dust swirled around his ankles. Lindani was happy because his mother would make medicine with the herbs he'd found to cure sore heads and bruises. She was teaching him how to make medicine, too.

Suddenly, a figure crashed into Lindani at full speed and he was thrown to the ground. The bag he was carrying landed in the dust.

"Ow! Busani, what do you think you're doing?"
Lindani cried out, as he picked himself up.
"Honestly, you're crazy, crazy."

Lindani glared at his brother. It was like looking
into a mirror, except his reflection was laughing
like a hyena. Despite the fact he was covered in dust
and grass from being wrestled to the ground
by his twin brother, Lindani started
laughing as well.

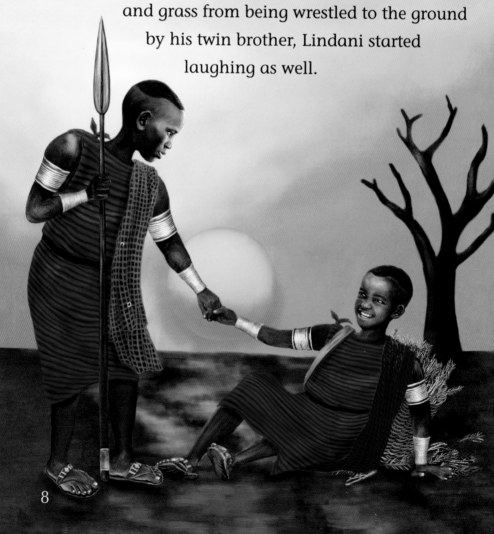

"Let's go hunting, Lindani. I'm bored with doing chores and I can't go hunting without you because you've got the best tracking skills," begged Busani, grabbing his twin in a headlock.

Busani was taller, stronger and more confident than his brother. Lindani used his brains to get things done, but he was quiet and shy. He was even scared of the village girls!

"If I can pin you down, will you come with me?" taunted Busani. Lindani smiled at the challenge. They both knew who'd win.

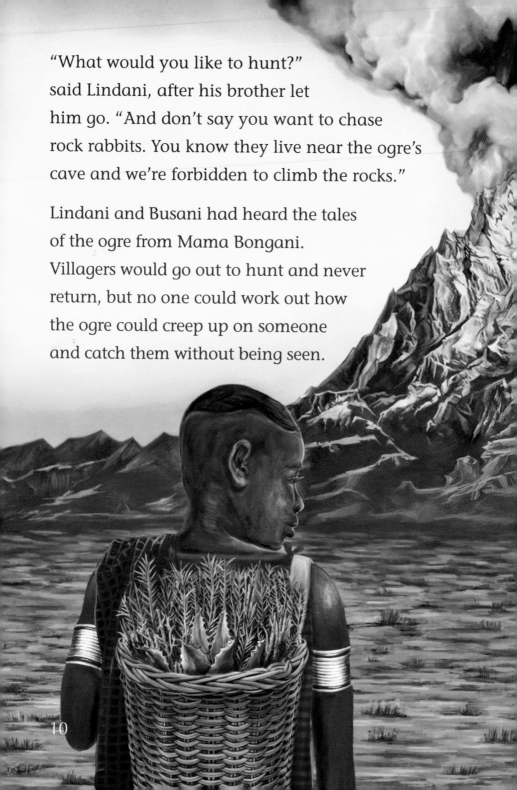

"What would you like to hunt?"
said Lindani, after his brother let
him go. "And don't say you want to chase
rock rabbits. You know they live near the ogre's
cave and we're forbidden to climb the rocks."

Lindani and Busani had heard the tales
of the ogre from Mama Bongani.
Villagers would go out to hunt and never
return, but no one could work out how
the ogre could creep up on someone
and catch them without being seen.

The boys turned to face
the mountain which towered
above them. Dark clouds draped
over the peak, and little sparks of
fire were shooting through the top.
The ogre wasn't happy – there was
no mistaking that.

3 The tree

Lindani and Busani stopped suddenly. The sweat on their bodies shone in the midday sun and rolled down their faces into their eyes. Where was the antelope they'd been chasing for an hour? One minute it was there, and the next it seemed to disappear, like a shadow in the dark. And where had that enormous tree come from? They knew this area well and never before had they seen a tree this size.

Busani crept forward, his spear at the ready. Bursts of wind raced around the tree, running through the leaves and making the branches creak. "Come find your lost antelope," whispered the branches. "I have him here in my trunk. I've trapped him for you."

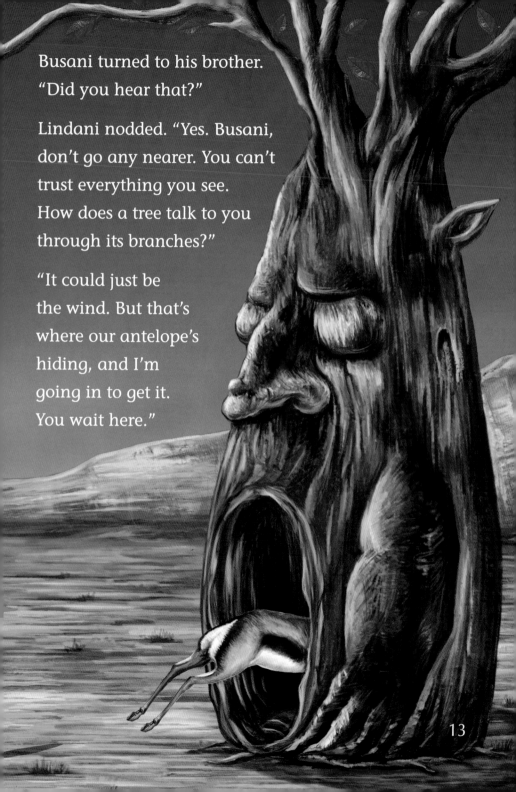

Busani turned to his brother.
"Did you hear that?"

Lindani nodded. "Yes. Busani,
don't go any nearer. You can't
trust everything you see.
How does a tree talk to you
through its branches?"

"It could just be
the wind. But that's
where our antelope's
hiding, and I'm
going in to get it.
You wait here."

13

Busani rushed at the tree. In a flash, the tree scooped him up into its branches!

Lindani gasped as, with one twist, the branches of the tree transformed into the ogre. It was so big, Lindani felt his body shaking with fear. So that was how the ogre managed to catch villagers – it could change its shape!

The ogre roared in triumph, and lumbered off in large, bone-shaking steps, with Busani grasped in one giant hand.

"Lindani, help me!" Busani's yells tore through the air, piercing Lindani's heart like an arrow.

"Busani!" Lindani ran after the ogre as fast as he could, but he couldn't catch it. He fell to the ground, trying to catch his breath, tears falling down his face.

Lindani could now only faintly hear Busani crying out for help. But there was nothing Lindani could do.

It was Mama Bongani who first saw Lindani return to the village alone. She saw the fear in Lindani's eyes and knew at once that the ogre had taken Busani. "Sipho, Zandile, come quick, hurry!" she screeched, as Lindani collapsed into her strong arms.

"I tried to get Busani back, but the tree was too big," Lindani cried.

Sipho took Lindani by the shoulders. "What do you mean – the tree was too big? Is Busani stuck in a tree?"

"No!" Lindani cried. "The ogre disguised itself as a tree and now it's got Busani!"

4 The potion

Many weeks passed. The ogre hadn't eaten Busani, oh no. It kept Busani on a lead and used the boy's hunting skills to capture animals for him. The ogre could've used its own magic to catch animals, but it was much too lazy and having Busani to do it was more fun. The ogre never allowed Busani to stray too far out of sight, and kept him chained up in a cave when he wasn't hunting.

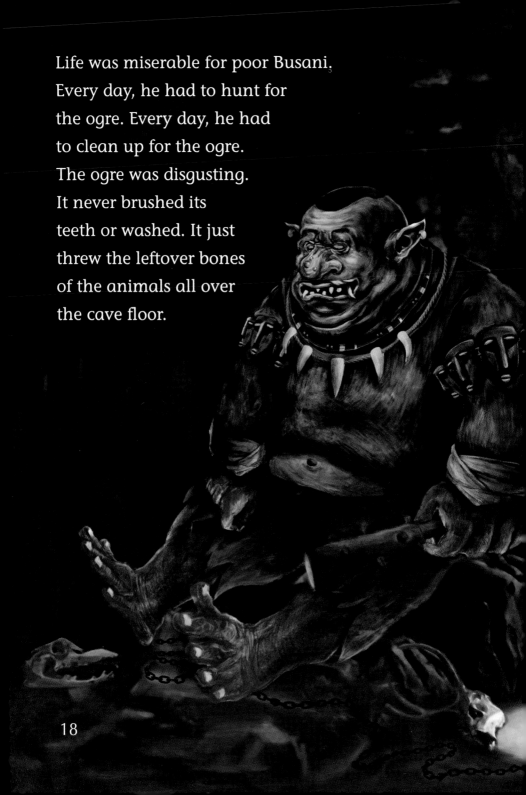

Life was miserable for poor Busani.
Every day, he had to hunt for
the ogre. Every day, he had
to clean up for the ogre.
The ogre was disgusting.
It never brushed its
teeth or washed. It just
threw the leftover bones
of the animals all over
the cave floor.

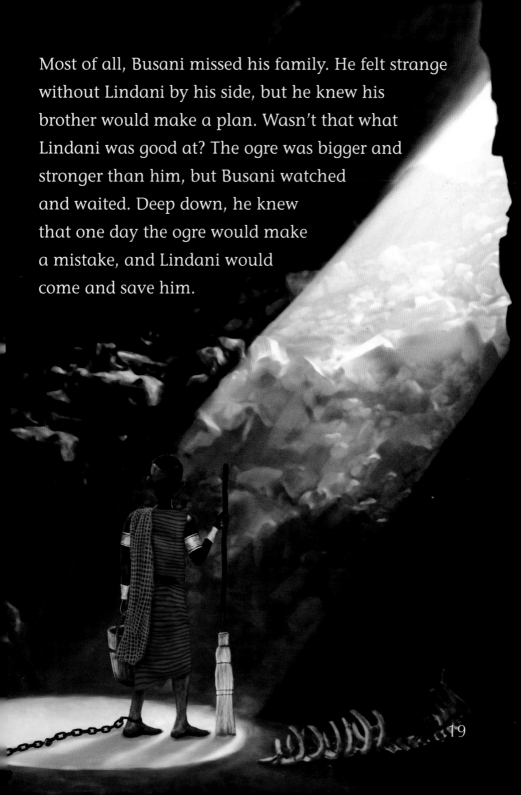

Most of all, Busani missed his family. He felt strange without Lindani by his side, but he knew his brother would make a plan. Wasn't that what Lindani was good at? The ogre was bigger and stronger than him, but Busani watched and waited. Deep down, he knew that one day the ogre would make a mistake, and Lindani would come and save him.

Since he returned to the village, Lindani had spent every day and every night working on plans to save his brother from the ogre.

First, he made a strong, sharp spear, but he knew he was no hunter like Busani. Then, he made a slingshot out of rope, but his aim wasn't very good. Then he remembered some of the herbs he'd collected for his mother. One of them was used to help people sleep.

What if he mixed an extra-strong sleeping potion for the ogre? He didn't know how he was going to get the ogre to drink it, but it was his best idea yet.

Lindani collected the herbs together and boiled them up with sweet-tasting berries. After boiling the mixture for a day and a night, he poured it into a wooden bottle and plugged it up with reeds.

Zandile didn't want to let him go, but Lindani smiled at his mother. "Can't you see I'm nearly a man? I'm strong and I feel in my heart that my brother isn't dead. He's alive and waiting for me, I know it!"

Lindani put the potion bottle into his bag, along with some food, and set off into the wilds.

5 The ogre

After two days and two nights, Lindani reached
the foot of the mountain. The rocks were black,
like jagged teeth waiting to tear at you if you slipped.
Lindani could see animal bones scattered amongst
the rocks.

This ogre has a large appetite, thought Lindani,
and he shifted the weight of the potion on his
skinny back. Let's hope it's just as thirsty.

Lindani was halfway up the mountain when …

"Hey, you BOY!" bellowed the ogre,
striding towards him.

Lindani froze, balancing on
the jagged rocks and trying
not to look at the long
drop below.

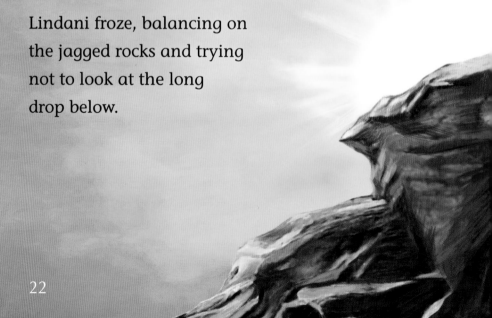

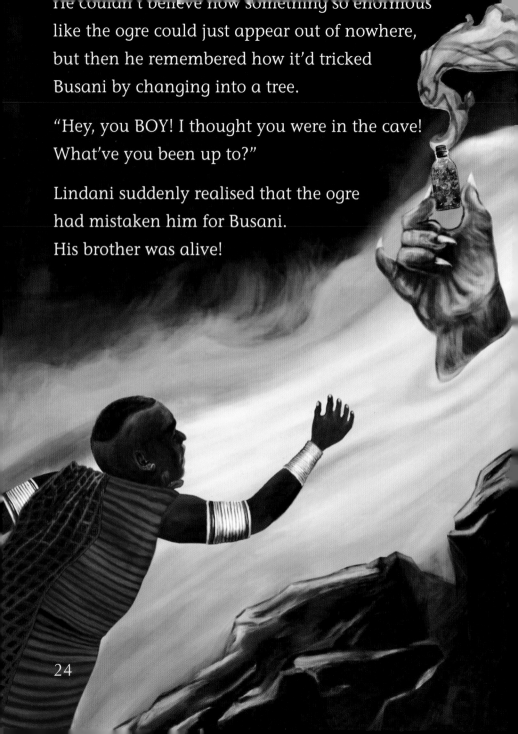

He couldn't believe how something so enormous like the ogre could just appear out of nowhere, but then he remembered how it'd tricked Busani by changing into a tree.

"Hey, you BOY! I thought you were in the cave! What've you been up to?"

Lindani suddenly realised that the ogre had mistaken him for Busani.
His brother was alive!

Taking a deep breath, Lindani turned to face the ogre. The stench from the ogre's breath nearly made Lindani topple over the edge of the rocks. He held on to a jagged edge and looked up into the ogre's small, crazed eyes.

"I've been making a special drink to go with your meal," whispered Lindani, trying not to stare too hard at the warts and sores covering the ogre's large face.

"Give it to me, BOY! I want to test it!" yelled the ogre, and it grabbed the potion out of the boy's trembling hands.

He glugged it back and the potion ran
down the sides of his mouth, over his
chin and on to his huge heaving chest.

The ogre smacked his lips. "Oh ho! This is delic – "

The potion had worked so well, and so quickly,
the ogre fell asleep immediately! It collapsed with
a thunderous crash, which made
the mountain shake and rattle.
Lindani couldn't believe
his luck.

He climbed round the ogre and up the side of the mountain, and found the entrance to the ogre's cave. Looking into the gloomy darkness, he called, "Hello?" He knew Busani was alive, but where was he? Suddenly, he saw a movement at the back of the cave. It was Busani!

"Lindani?" Busani dropped the shovel he was using to clean up, and ran to his brother's arms.

"I knew you were alive!" cried Lindani, as the twins hugged each other tight.

"Where's the ogre?" Busani asked.

"I made a sleeping potion," Lindani explained. "The ogre thought I was you, and drank it up! We need to leave now, before it wakes up."

The twins ran down the mountainside, balancing from rock to rock. But when they came to the place where the ogre had fallen asleep, it wasn't there.

"Look!" Busani pointed down the steep mountainside. Lindani looked. The ogre had rolled off the mountain while it was asleep, and now it lay dead at the bottom.

"The village will be free!" they said. Hand in hand, they made their way down towards home.

When the boys arrived back at their village, they were
greeted with song and laughter, led by Mama Bongani.
Zandile and Sipho hugged their children tight, tears
rolling down their cheeks.

The party that night was loud, but not as loud
as the sound of thunder, as the rain
began to fall again.

The Daily News

Twins defeat ogre!

The ogre, who lived in a cave at the top of the mountain, had been snatching villagers for years. It also drank up all the rain, leaving the village without water.

Tricked!

When Busani and Lindani were out hunting one day, Busani was tricked into climbing a tree. The tree was actually the ogre in disguise! It snatched Busani and carried him off to its cave.

Clever thinking

Lindani, who'd always helped his mother make medicines for the village, made a very powerful sleeping potion. He fooled the ogre, who drank the potion and fell fast asleep. After Lindani had bravely rescued his brother, they discovered the ogre had rolled to the bottom of the mountain.

Weather Forecast

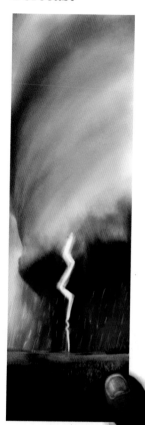

The ogre is dead!

The village is now free from the ogre. A friend of the family, Mama Bongani, told the Daily News, "I knew those boys were special."

OGRE

Ideas for reading

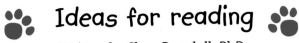

Written by Clare Dowdall, PhD
Lecturer and Primary Literacy Consultant

Reading objectives:
- use dictionaries to check the meaning of words
- discuss their understanding and explain the meaning of words in context
- draw inferences and justify these with evidence
- make predictions from details stated and applied

Spoken language objectives:
- use spoken language to develop understanding through speculating, hypothesising, imagining and exploring ideas

Curriculum links: Geography - Africa

Resources: ICT for research; art materials; pens and paper

Build a context for reading
- Show children the word "ogre" on a whiteboard. Ask children what an ogre is, and share ideas about films and stories that feature ogres.
- Look at the image on the front cover. Ask children to discuss what they can see, and where they think the story is set.
- Read the blurb. Focus on the word "fearsome" and check that children understand it.

Understand and apply reading strategies
- Ask for a volunteer to read pp2–4 aloud whilst the other children close their eyes and imagine what it would be like to live where it doesn't rain and there isn't enough to drink.
- Encourage children to share their ideas of what it would be like. Explain that this is an African story.
- Read on to p6 together. Ask children to make inferences and deductions about how Lindani and Busani are going to be special, and why it rained when they were born.